THE GAMEMASTER

written by John Bochak

illustrated by Grayce Bochak

Simon & Schuster Books for Young Readers

SIMON & SCHUSTER BOOKS FOR YOUNG READERS
An imprint of Simon & Schuster Children's Publishing Division
1230 Avenue of the Americas
New York, NY 10020

Designed by Christy Hale
The text of this book is set in Windsor Light.
The illustrations are rendered in cut paper.
Printed in United States of America

10 9 8 7 6 5 4 3 2 1

Library of Congress Cataloging-in-Publication Data
Bochak, John. The Gamemaster / story by John Bochak; pictures by Grayce Bochak.
—1st American ed. p. cm. Summary: A boy who loves to play games lives out a fantastic
adventure when the pieces of his chessboard come to life one night.
ISBN: 0-689-80292-7
[1. Fantasy. 2. Chess—Fiction.] I. Bochak, Grayce, ill. II. Title.
PZ7.B6535Gam 1995
[Fic]—dc20 94-14182

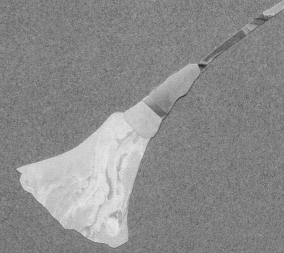

*To all those who
love a good game*

I t happened at night, when the pale white light of
the moon passed through my window and onto the old
game box in the corner of my bedroom. I would tiptoe
over and quietly open the box, waiting for the sound.
WHOOOOOOSSSHHHH . . .
WHOOOOOOSSSHHHH . . .
WHOOOOOOSSSHHHH . . .
A great wind would sweep out and carry me into,
around, and through. . . .

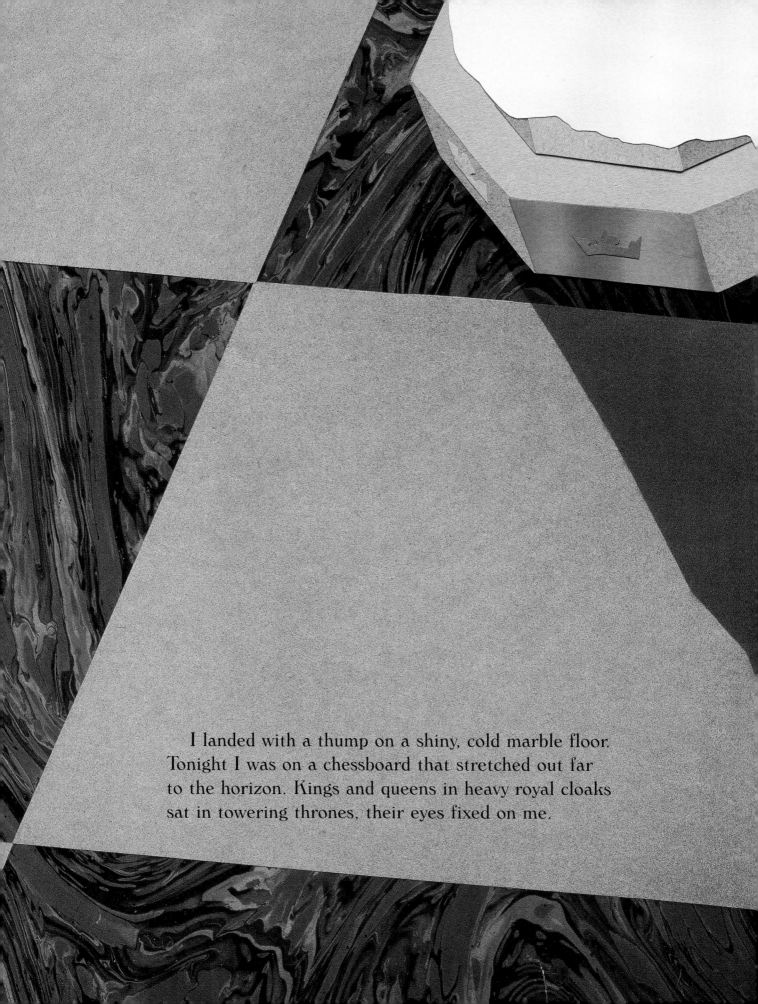

I landed with a thump on a shiny, cold marble floor.
Tonight I was on a chessboard that stretched out far
to the horizon. Kings and queens in heavy royal cloaks
sat in towering thrones, their eyes fixed on me.

A voice thundered out,
"Why are you here, young boy?"
"I love to play games," I answered.
"Do you have a game for me tonight?"

The kings and queens lowered their heads and whispered to one another.

One of the kings, with a voice so loud it shook the floor, said, "If it's games you love, then find the Gamemaster. He is brave as a knight, clever as a rook, strong as a pawn, wise as a bishop, and noble as a king or queen." He lifted his thick, gray eyebrow and warned, "You must find him before all the stars vanish in the morning sky, or remain here never to return home."

With a bow to the king, as in the stories of long ago, I agreed.

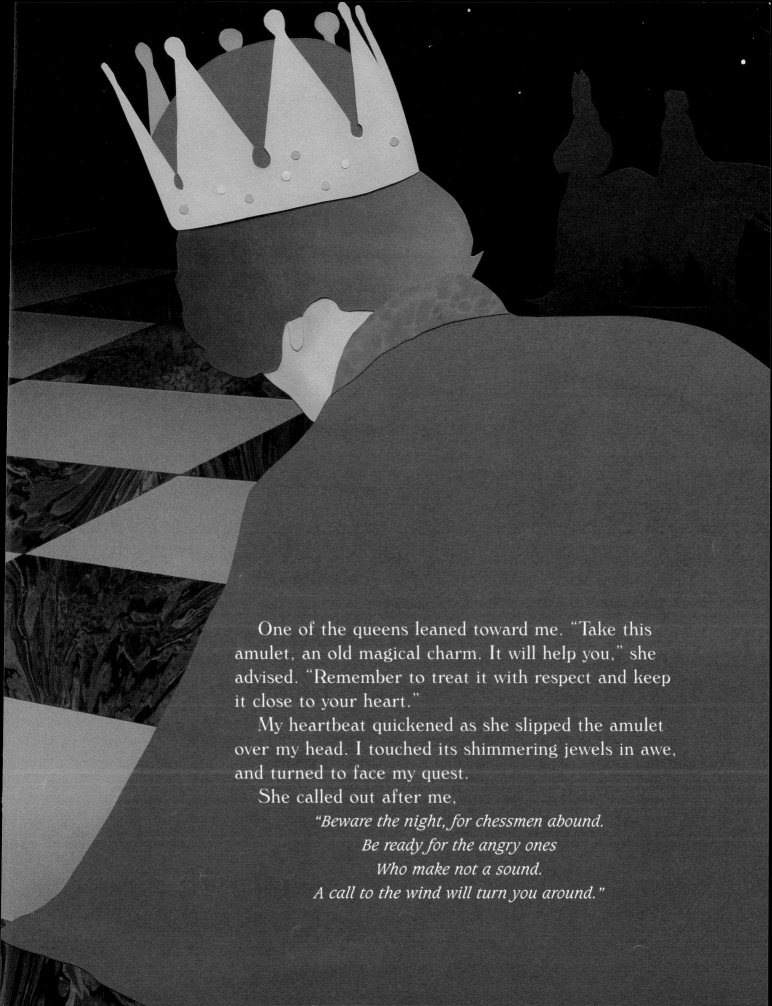

One of the queens leaned toward me. "Take this amulet, an old magical charm. It will help you," she advised. "Remember to treat it with respect and keep it close to your heart."

My heartbeat quickened as she slipped the amulet over my head. I touched its shimmering jewels in awe, and turned to face my quest.

She called out after me,

> *"Beware the night, for chessmen abound.*
> *Be ready for the angry ones*
> *Who make not a sound.*
> *A call to the wind will turn you around."*

I could feel the royals staring hard at me as I crept out to the unknown world. Before long, I felt a chill. The air smelled of a thousand years.

The stillness was broken as something brushed close to my side. Suddenly, wild-eyed men surrounded me with raised shields. I gave a furious shout. "Which one of you is the Gamemaster?"

The boldest, his huge arm raised for battle, answered, "None of us! We are pawns, foot soldiers quick to anger and ready to fight." His powerful voice boomed,

"Fool the fellow with a bag of gold,
A jewel for him, a jewel for you.
Show us your strength and break our hold,
Then your game will begin to unfold."

I clenched my fists tightly and, with a mighty push, hurled myself through the circle of raging soldiers and slipped far into the darkness.

Strange sounds were all around. I heard a scurrying of feet from the left, then jingling from the right. Greedy-looking ones jumped out at me, the heat of their breath on my face. One reached with his hand, like a snake striking out, to snatch the amulet. I pulled back on the old charm. "Thieves!" I cried. "Tell me where the Gamemaster is hiding!"

One of the men grinned. "We are rooks, cunning fellows who want something for that answer," he demanded. My hands trembled as I offered the smallest jewel from the amulet, fearing the queen's disapproval.

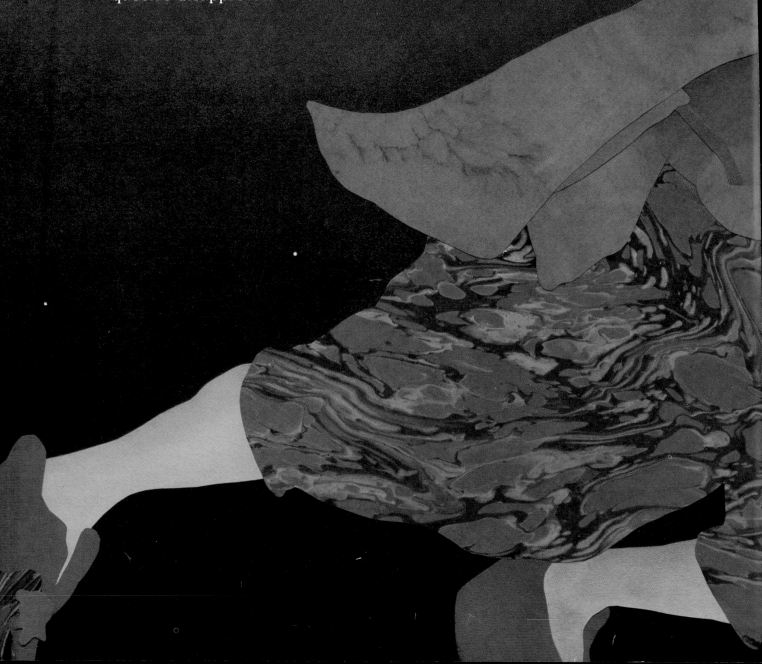

As soon as the jewel was in his grasp, the quick-footed rooks escaped with the treasure and left not a clue. I hung my head low. For this I had sacrificed a piece of the charm! Then, out of the corner of my eye, I glimpsed a tattered piece of paper drifting to the ground. I reached for it and read,

"Where the moon doesn't shine, that's where to look.
Be clever tonight—find a horseman on foot.
Don't give up now, there are clues to be found.
Don't let the wind yet turn you around."

I prowled, paced, dashed, and darted
through the darkness, weaving my way
toward fading, distant sounds. Finally, I
heard the approaching *thud-a-dud, thud-a-dud*
of horses' hooves echoing against the marble
floor. The Gamemaster! Running fast to follow
the sound, I came to a place where ghostly figures
of horsemen lurked in the mist.
"Surely one of you is the Gamemaster!" I called out.

The one on foot knelt down and told me, "We are
knights, fearless and gallant men." Resting his heavy
hand on my shoulder, he said,
> "Walk farther alone into the night, or
> Ride with us but show no fright.
> Men with beards of gray, white, and tan,
> Find the oldest if you can."

With a great leap onto the knight's horse, I
wrapped the reins tightly around my hands and
shouted, "Now I am the youngest knight of all!"

I rode with a fury, breathing air filled with ancient
dust. The horsemen followed closely, howling with
rage. Seconds turned to minutes . . . minutes turned
to hours. . . . When I dared to look back, no knights
could be seen through the lowering fog. Pulling back
hard on the reins, I brought the horse to a halt.

Someone else was lurking there.

Out of the haze, four bearded men appeared and
looked at me with piercing eyes. Slipping off the horse,
I stood before the one with a beard so white. "Sir, might
you be the Gamemaster?" I asked, in nearly a whisper.
He shook his head and answered, "We are bishops,
men who unravel mysteries." Hobbling closer, he chanted,

"Boy so young and boy so wise,
Look for the dust between earth and sky.
You hold the charm that tells no lie.
The answer is in this night's quest.
You're the one who knows it best."

The bishops gestured with open palms. They
wanted something for the melodious song.

I gave them the golden cord from the amulet.
Happily, they danced away, two by two, their voices
drifting eerily into the mist. I was alone.

I saw the stars begin to vanish and the sky start to brighten, and I remembered what the king and queen had warned. Had I cursed myself by giving up the amulet's jewel and cord?

I turned the amulet over in my hands, wondering of its power. "Where is this Gamemaster I must find?" I asked the old charm with a sigh.

My eyes widened. Dust! It covered the underside of the amulet, the side that had been closest to my heart. *The dust between earth and sky,* I thought as I rubbed it away. My own reflection stared back at me. A mirror! "That's it. . . ."

"I have been the one who was brave, noble, and clever, wise, and strong in this game tonight!" Raising the amulet high in the sky, I gave a triumphant shout.

"I am the Gamemaster! This game is won.
I challenge you kings to a game twice the fun.
Tomorrow night may cost you the crown.
Come, great wind, and turn me around!"

Closing my eyes tightly, ready to return home,
a wind swirled and swept me back, around and
through. . . .

I felt the morning sun against my face. All the game pieces stood silent on the board. But deep within the box, I thought I heard the distant roar of another great wind stirring.